The Winter Fox

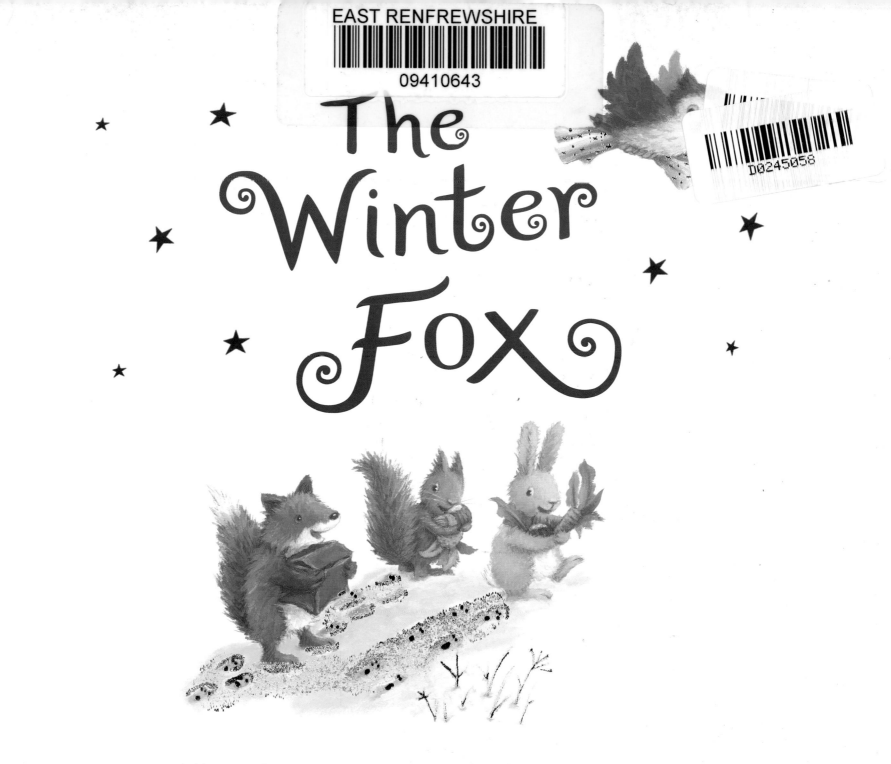

Timothy Knapman • Rebecca Harry

nosy crow

Once there was a fox who played all summer long.

"Summer is nearly over!" called Fox.
"Come and play while the sun is shining!"
But his friends were all too busy.

"Winter is coming!" they said.
"We have work to do!"

The friends were worried about Fox.
What would happen to him
when winter came?

"Let me help you, Fox," said Rabbit. "I can show you just the right place to build a home. Then you will be near us all winter long."

But Fox didn't listen. He was too busy rolling around on the soft carpet of flowers.

So Owl tried to help.
"I can show you how to
make a cosy bed," she said.
"Then you will be snuggly
and warm all winter long."

But Fox didn't listen.
He was too busy splashing in the lake.

Next, it was Squirrel's turn to try. "I can show you how to store up food," he said. "Then you will have plenty to eat **all** winter long."

But Fox **still** didn't listen. He was **too busy** chasing butterflies.

"Winter is coming," said Fox's friends. "The white snow will fall and the freezing wind will blow. We will be tucked up till spring, but what will **you** do?"

"I will play in the snow and sing to the wind and
have the whole forest to myself!" said Fox.
"Now come and have fun!"

But the other animals had **work** to do,
while Fox just played all through the autumn.

And then winter came.
The white snow fell and
the freezing wind blew.

Rabbit had his cosy home in just the right place.
Owl had her warm and snuggly nest.
And Squirrel had lots of tasty
acorns to eat.

They were all ready for winter. But what about Fox?

Poor Fox was too cold to play
in the snow, too hungry to sing
to the wind and he was all on
his own in the frozen forest.

"Oh, I wish I'd listened
to my friends," thought Fox.

"I wish, I wish . . ."

Fox looked up for a star
to wish upon.

And the more he wished, the bigger the star grew.
It grew bigger and bigger and bigger until . . .

. . . BONK!

It hit him on the head!
"Ouch!" said Fox.
But the star wasn't a star
at all! It was a box wrapped
in shiny, silver paper.

Fox could have kept it
all to himself . . .

The box had broken
open and out spilled toys
and food and bright things
that sparkled in the snow.

. . . but he had a better idea.

Quickly, he piled everything back into the box
and set off. He had **work** to do!

The next morning,
Rabbit, Owl and Squirrel
found wonderful gifts
outside their homes.

"Where did it all
come from?"
they wondered.

Then they spotted a trail
of paw prints in the snow,
and followed them **all** the way to . . .

. . . Fox! He had a great feast laid out for them.

"Presents and now this!" said the friends.
"Thank you, Fox!"

"You all tried to help me before,
but I wouldn't listen," said Fox. "I'm sorry."

When they couldn't eat anything more,
the animals played in the snow
and sang to the wind.

They chased snowflakes, went sliding across the frozen lake and rolled on the soft carpet of snow.

At last, it started to get dark and Rabbit said, "It's nearly time for bed, Fox. Why don't you come back with us?"

So the four friends packed everything up and walked off through the forest.

As the moon rose above them,
the friends reached the big oak tree.

"See, Fox," said Rabbit,
"if you build your home here,
you will be near us all winter long.
It's just the right place."

"And if you make a cosy bed
from this box and paper," said Owl,
"you can be snuggly and warm
when the freezing wind blows."

"And look, if you store up these leftovers,"
said Squirrel, "you will have plenty
to eat until the white snow melts."

And for once, Fox did listen.
"Thank you," he said. "You are such good friends."

Now Fox had
everything he needed.

And he was never **cold**, or **hungry**,
or **lonely** ever again.

In loving memory of my grandpa, Tom Davies xxx – R.H.

To Annie, Florence and Clementine, with love – T.K.

First published in 2016 by Nosy Crow Ltd
The Crow's Nest, 10a Lant Street
London SE1 1QR
www.nosycrow.com

ISBN 978 0 85763 396 5 (HB)
ISBN 978 0 85763 706 2 (PB)

Nosy Crow and associated logos are trademarks
and/or registered trademarks of Nosy Crow Ltd.

Text copyright © Timothy Knapman 2016
Illustrations copyright © Rebecca Harry 2016

The right of Timothy Knapman to be identified as the author of this work, and of
Rebecca Harry to be identified as the illustrator of this work has been asserted.

A CIP catalogue record for this book is available from the British Library.

Printed in China
Papers used by Nosy Crow are made from wood grown in sustainable forests.

1 3 5 7 9 8 6 4 2 (HB)
1 3 5 7 9 8 6 4 2 (PB)